KATE GREENAWAY

NURSERY RHYME CLASSICS

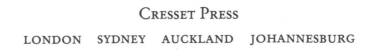

CRESSET PRESS

LONDON   SYDNEY   AUCKLAND   JOHANNESBURG

First published in 1988

This impression published in 1991 by
Cresset Press an imprint of the
Random House UK
20 Vauxhall Bridge Road
London SW1V 2SA

Designed by Polly Dawes
Edited by Alison Sage

ISBN 0 7126 3464 9

Printed and bound in China

CONTENTS

STRANGE
AND
WONDERFUL

HARK! HARK! THE DOGS DO BARK

Hark! Hark! The dogs do bark,
The beggars are coming to town;
Some in rags and some in tags,
And some in silken gowns.

Some gave them white bread
And some gave them brown,
Some gave them plum cake
And drummed them out of town.

RIDE A COCK-HORSE

Ride a cock-horse to Banbury Cross
To see a fine lady on a white horse,
Rings on her fingers, bells on her toes;
She shall have music wherever she goes.

SING A SONG OF SIXPENCE

Sing a song of sixpence,
A pocket full of rye,
Four-and-twenty blackbirds
Baked in a pie;
When the pie was opened
The birds began to sing;
Wasn't that a dainty dish
To set before a king?

The King was in his counting house
Counting out his money,
The Queen was in the parlour
Eating bread and honey;
The maid was in the garden
Hanging out the clothes,
When down flew a blackbird
And pecked off her nose.

THERE WAS AN OLD WOMAN
LIVED UNDER A HILL

There was an old woman lived under a hill;
And if she's not gone, she lives there still.
Baked apples she sells and gooseberry pies,
She's the old woman who never tells lies.

THE MAN IN THE WILDERNESS

The man in the wilderness asked me,
How many strawberries grew in the sea;
I answered him, as I thought good,
As many red herrings as grow in a wood.

LITTLE TOMMY TUCKER

Little Tommy Tucker,
He sang for his supper.
What did he sing for?
Why, white bread and butter.
How can I cut it without a knife?
How can I marry without a wife?

GOOSEY, GOOSEY GANDER

Goosey, goosey gander, whither shall I wander?
Upstairs and downstairs and in my lady's chamber.
There I met an old man who wouldn't say his prayers;
Take him by the left leg and throw him down the stairs.

HALF A POUND OF TWOPENNY RICE

Half a pound of twopenny rice,
Half a pound of treacle.
That's the way the money goes,
Pop goes the weasel!

In and out the city gates
Up and down the Eagle.
That's the way the money goes,
Pop goes the weasel!

HUMPTY DUMPTY SAT
ON THE WALL

Humpty Dumpty sat on the wall
Humpty Dumpty had a great fall.
All the King's horses and all the King's men
Couldn't put Humpty together again.

RING-A-RING-A-ROSES

Ring-a-ring-a-roses
A pocket full of posies.
Atishoo! Atishoo!
We all fall down.

Picking up the daisies
Picking up the daisies.
Atishoo! Atishoo!
We all stand up.

I HAD A LITTLE NUT TREE

I had a little nut tree and nothing would it bear
But a silver nutmeg and a golden pear.
The King of Spain's daughter came to visit me
And all for the sake of my little nut tree.
I danced over the water, I danced over the sea
But all the birds of the air couldn't catch me.

IF ALL THE WORLD WAS APPLE PIE

If all the world was apple pie
And all the sea was ink
And all the trees were bread and cheese
What should we have to drink?

THE GRAND OLD DUKE OF YORK

Oh, the grand old Duke of York,
He had ten thousand men;
He marched them up to the top of the hill
And he marched them down again.
And when they were up, they were up,
And when they were down, they were down,
And when they were only halfway up,
They were neither up nor down.

HOW MANY MILES TO BABYLON?

How many miles to Babylon?
Three score and ten.
Can I get there by candlelight?
Yes, and back again.
If your heels are nimble and light,
You may get there by candlelight.

OLD MOTHER GOOSE

Old Mother Goose, when
She wanted to wander,
Would ride through the air
On a very fine gander.

She had a son Jack,
A nice-looking lad,
He was not very good
Nor yet very bad.

She sent him to market,
A live goose he bought.
'Here, Mother,' says he,
'It won't go for nought.'

Jack's goose and the gander
Grew very fond,
They'd both eat together,
Or swim in one pond.

Jack found, one fine morning,
As I have been told,
His goose had laid him
An egg of pure gold.

SALLY GO ROUND THE SUN

Sally go round the sun
Sally go round the moon
Sally go round the chimney pots
On a Saturday afternoon.

I SAW THREE SHIPS

I saw three ships come sailing by
On New Year's Day in the morning.

And what do you think was in them, then,
On New Year's Day in the morning?

Three pretty girls were in them, then,
On New Year's Day in the morning.

And one could whistle and one could sing,
And one could play on the violin –
Such joy there was at my wedding,
On New Year's Day in the morning.

THERE WAS AN OLD WOMAN
TOSSED UP IN A BASKET

There was an old woman tossed up in a basket
Ninety-nine times as high as the moon;
And what she did there, I couldn't but ask it,
For in her hand she carried a broom.
'Old woman, old woman, old woman,' said I,
'What are you doing up there so high?'
'I'm sweeping the cobwebs out of the sky
And you can come with me, by and by.'

ONE FOR SORROW,
TWO FOR JOY

One for sorrow, two for joy,
Three for a girl and four for a boy;
Five for silver,
Six for gold
And seven for a secret that's never been told.

BIRDS
AND
BEASTS

DIDDLY, DIDDLY, DUMPTY,

Diddly, diddly, dumpty,
The cat ran up the plum tree,
Give her a plum and down she'll come,
Diddly, diddly, dumpty.

TO MARKET TO MARKET

To market to market to buy a fat pig,
Home again, home again jiggerty jig.
To market to market to buy a plum bun,
Home again, home again market is done.

LITTLE BO PEEP

Little Bo Peep has lost her sheep
And can't tell where to find them.
Leave them alone and they'll come home
And bring their tails behind them.

Little Bo Peep fell fast asleep
And dreamed she heard them bleating;
But when she awoke she found it a joke
For they were still a-fleeting.

Then up she took her little crook,
Determined for to find them;
She found them indeed, but it made her heart bleed,
For they'd left their tails behind them.

It happened one day as Bo Peep did stray
Over a meadow close by,
That there she espied their tails side by side,
All hung on a tree to dry.

She heaved a sigh and wiped her eye
And over the hills went rambling.
She tried what she could, as a shepherdess should,
To tack each again to its lambkin.

LADYBIRD,
LADYBIRD FLY AWAY HOME!

Ladybird, ladybird
Fly away home!
Your house is on fire
And your children are gone!

TWO LITTLE DICKY BIRDS

Two little dicky birds sitting on a wall,
One called Peter, one called Paul.
Fly away Peter! Fly away Paul!
Come back Peter! Come back Paul!

LITTLE MISS MUFFET

Little Miss Muffet
Sat on a tuffet
Eating some curds and whey;
There came a great spider
And sat down beside her
And frightened Miss Muffet away.

INCY WINCY SPIDER,
CLIMBING UP THE SPOUT

Incy wincy spider, climbing up the spout
Down came the rain, and washed the spider out.
Out came the sun and dried up all the rain,
Incy wincy spider climbed up the spout again.

DING DONG BELL

Ding dong bell,
Pussy's in the well.
Who put her in?
Little Tommy Thin.
Who pulled her out?
Little Johnny Stout.
What a naughty boy was that
To hurt poor pussy cat
Who never did any harm
But killed all the mice in his father's barn.

I SAW A LITTLE BIRD

I saw a little bird
Come hop, hop, hop;
So I cried, 'Little bird,
Will you stop, stop, stop?'
I opened the window
To say, 'How do you do?'
But he shook his little tail
And away he flew.

ONE, TWO, THREE, FOUR, FIVE

One, two, three, four, five,
Once I caught a fish alive.
Six, seven, eight, nine, ten,
Then I put it back again.
'Why did you let it go?'
'Because it bit my finger so.'
'Which finger did it bite?'
'This little finger on my right.'

WHO KILLED COCK ROBIN?

Who killed Cock Robin?
'I,' said the Sparrow,
'With my bow and arrow,
I killed Cock Robin.'

Who saw him die?
'I,' said the Fly,
'With my little eye,
I saw him die.'

Who'll dig his grave?
'I,' said the Owl,
'With my spade and trowel,
I'll dig his grave.'

Who'll be the parson?
'I,' said the Rook,
'With my bell and book,
I'll be the parson.'

Who'll toll the bell?
'I,' said the Bull,
'Because I can pull,
I'll toll the bell.'

All the birds of the air
Fell to sighing and to sobbing
When they heard of the death of poor Cock Robin,
When they heard of the death of poor Cock Robin.

HIGGLEDY PIGGLEDY, MY FAT HEN

Higgledy piggledy, my fat hen,
She lays eggs for gentlemen.
Gentlemen come every day
To see what my fat hen can lay.

PUSSY CAT, PUSSY CAT

'Pussy cat, pussy cat where have you been?'
'I've been up to London to visit the Queen.'
'Pussy cat, pussy cat, what did you there?'
'I frightened a little mouse under her chair.'

I LOVE LITTLE PUSSY

I love little pussy, her coat is so warm
And if I don't hurt her she'll do me no harm.
So I won't pull her tail, nor drive her away,
But pussy and I together will play.
She will sit by my side
And I'll give her some food;
And pussy will love me because I am good.

BAA, BAA BLACK SHEEP

'Baa, baa black sheep
Have you any wool?'
'Yes, sir, yes, sir.
Three bags full.
One for the master,
One for the dame
And one for the little boy
Who lives down the lane.'

MARY HAD A LITTLE LAMB

Mary had a little lamb,
Its fleece was white as snow
And everywhere that Mary went
The lamb was sure to go.

It followed her to school one day,
Which was against the rule;
It made the children laugh and play
To see a lamb at school.

And so the teacher sent it out,
But still it waited near;
And stood there patiently about
Till Mary did appear.

'Why does the lamb love Mary so?'
The eager children cry;
'Why, Mary loves the lamb, you know,'
The teacher did reply.

WHERE, OH, WHERE HAS MY LITTLE DOG GONE?

Where, oh, where has my little dog gone?
Oh, where, oh, where can he be?
With his ears so short and his tail so long,
Oh, where, oh, where is he?

WORDS
OF
ADVICE

ELSIE MARLEY

Elsie Marley's grown so fine
She won't get up to feed the swine
But lays in bed till half past nine!
Lazy Elsie Marley.

THERE WAS A LITTLE GIRL

There was a little girl
And she had a little curl
Right in the middle of her forehead.
When she was good
She was very, very good,
But when she was bad, she was horrid.

WHAT ARE LITTLE BOYS MADE OF?

What are little boys made of?
What are little boys made of?
Frogs and snails
And puppy dogs' tails;
That's what little boys are made of.

What are little girls made of?
What are little girls made of?
Sugar and spice
And all things nicc;
That's what little girls are made of.

MATTHEW, MARK, LUKE AND JOHN

Matthew, Mark, Luke and John
Bless the bed that I lie on.
Four corners to my bed
Four angels round my head.
One to sing and one to pray
And two to carry my soul away.

RED SKY AT NIGHT

Red sky at night
Shepherd's delight.
Red sky in the morning
Shepherd's warning.

HE LOVES ME, HE LOVES ME NOT

He loves me,
He loves me not,
He loves me,
He loves me not.

Counting blossoms on the tree
How shall Daisy married be?

Tinker, tailor, soldier, sailor
Rich man, poor man, beggar man, thief.

FRIDAY'S DREAM

Friday's dream
On Saturday told
Is sure to come true
Be it never so old.

MARCH WINDS, APRIL SHOWERS

March winds, April showers
Bring forth May flowers.

A SUNSHINY SHOWER

A sunshiny shower
Won't last half-an-hour.
Rain before seven,
Fine before eleven.

THE FAIR MAID

The fair maid, who, the First of May
Goes to the fields at the break of day
And washes in dew from the hawthorn tree
Will ever after handsome be.

EARLY TO BED
AND EARLY TO RISE

Early to bed and early to rise
Makes children healthy, wealthy and wise.

MONDAY'S CHILD

Monday's child is fair of face;

Tuesday's child is full of grace;

Wednesday's child is full of woe;

Thursday's child has far to go;

Friday's child is loving and giving;

Saturday's child must work for a living,

But the child who is born on the Sabbath day
Is bonny and blithe and good and gay.

RAIN, RAIN, GO AWAY

Rain, rain, go away
Come again another day.
Rain, rain, go to Spain
And please don't come back here again.

LITTLE POLLY FLINDERS

Little Polly Flinders
Sat among the cinders,
Warming her pretty little toes;
Her mother came and caught her
And smacked her little daughter
For spoiling her nice new clothes.

GEORGIE PORGIE, PUDDING AND PIE

Georgie Porgie, pudding and pie,
Kissed the girls and made them cry.
When the girls begin to play
Georgie Porgie runs away.

One Foot Up And One Foot Down

One foot up and one foot down
This is the way to London Town.

ALL WORK AND NO PLAY

All work and no play
Makes Jack a dull boy.
All play and no work
Makes Jack just a toy.

ROW, ROW, ROW THE BOAT

Row, row, row the boat
Gently down the stream,
Merrily, merrily, merrily, merrily,
Life is but a dream.

COME, BUTTER, COME!

Come, butter, come!
Sarah stands at the garden gate
Waiting for a butter cake,
Come, butter, come!

SEE A PIN

See a pin and pick it up
And all the day you'll have good luck.
See a pin and let it lie
Wish you'll not have cause to cry.

DAISIES ARE OUR SILVER

Daisies are our silver
Buttercups our gold
I'd not exchange these glowing flowers
For heaps of wealth untold.

A DILLAR, A DOLLAR

A dillar, a dollar,
A ten o'clock scholar,
What makes you come so soon?
You used to come at ten o'clock
But now you come at noon.

ONE, TWO, THREE, FOUR

One, two, three, four,
Mary at the cottage door;
Five, six, seven, eight,
Eating cherries off a plate.

DO YOU KNOW THE MUFFIN MAN?

Do you known the muffin man
Do you know the muffin man
Do you know the muffin man
Who lives in Drury Lane?

Yes, I know the muffin man
Yes, I know the muffin man
Yes, I know the muffin man
Who lives in Drury Lane.

TOM, TOM THE PIPER'S SON

Tom, Tom the piper's son
Stole a pig and away did run.
The pig was eat
And Tom was beat
And he went roaring down the street.

MY MOTHER SAID, I NEVER SHOULD

My mother said, I never should
Play with the gypsies in the wood.
If I did, then she would say,
'Naughty girl to disobey.
Your hair shan't curl and your shoes won't shine.
You gypsy girl, you won't be mine.'

The wood was dark, the grass was green,
By came Sally with a tambourine.
I went to sea - no ship to get across,
So I paid a shilling for a blind white horse;
I upped on his back and was off in a crack –
Sally tell my mother that I'm never coming back.

HOT CROSS BUNS

Hot cross buns!
Hot cross buns!
One a penny, two a penny
Hot cross buns!

If you have no daughters,
Give them to your sons;
One a penny, two a penny
Hot cross buns!

HERE IS THE TREE
WITH LEAVES SO GREEN

Here is the tree with leaves so green,
Here are ripe apples that hang between,
When the wind blows,
The apples do fall
Into a basket which gathers them all.

LITTLE BOYS
AND
LITTLE GIRLS

LITTLE JACK HORNER

Little Jack Horner
Sat in the corner
Eating his Christmas pie;
He put in his thumb
And pulled out a plum
And said, 'What a good boy am I!'

DAFFY-DOWN-DILLY

Daffy-down-dilly has come up to town
In a yellow petticoat
And a green gown.

JACK SPRAT COULD EAT NO FAT

Jack Sprat could eat no fat
And his wife could eat no lean
And so between them both, you see,
They licked the platter clean.

LUCY LOCKET

Lucy Locket lost her pocket
Kitty Fisher found it;
There was not a penny in it,
But a ribbon round it.

CROSS PATCH

Cross Patch lift the latch
Sit by the fire and spin;
Take a cup and drink it up,
Then call your neighbours in.

WHERE ARE YOU GOING TO?

'Where are you going to, my pretty maid?'
'I'm going a-milking, sir,' she said.

'May I go with you, my pretty maid?'
'You're kindly welcome, sir,' she said.

'What is your father, my pretty maid?'
'My father's a farmer, sir,' she said.

'What is your fortune, my pretty maid?'
'My face is my fortune, sir,' she said.

'Then I can't marry you, my pretty maid,'
'Nobody asked you, sir,' she said.

POLLY PUT THE KETTLE ON

Polly put the kettle on
Polly put the kettle on;
We'll all have tea.

Sukie take if off again
Sukie take if off again
They've all gone away.

DRAW A PAIL OF WATER

Draw a pail of water
For my lady's daughter;
My father's a king and my mother's a queen
My two little sisters are dressed all in green;
Stamping grass and parsley
Marigold leaves and daisies;
One rush! Two rush!
Pray thee, fine lady come under my bush.

JACK AND JILL

Jack and Jill went up the hill
To fetch a pail of water.
Jack fell down
And broke his crown
And Jill came tumbling after.

Up Jack got and home did trot
As fast as he could caper.
He went to bed and wrapped his head
In vinegar and brown paper.

LITTLE TOMMY TITTLEMOUSE

Little Tommy Tittlemouse
Lived in a little house;
He caught fishes
In other men's ditches.

WILLY BOY, WILLY BOY,

'Willy boy, Willy boy, where are you going?
I will go with you, if I may.'
'I'm going to the meadow to see them a-mowing
I'm going to the meadow to make the new hay.'

CURLY LOCKS, CURLY LOCKS

Curly locks, curly locks will you be mine?
You shan't wash the dishes, nor yet feed the swine;
But sit on a cushion and sew a fine seam
And you shall eat strawberries, sugar and cream.

MARY, MARY, QUITE CONTRARY

Mary, Mary, quite contrary
How does your garden grow?
With silver bells
And cockle shells
And pretty maids all in a row.

LITTLE BOY BLUE

Little Boy Blue, come blow up your horn!
The sheep's in the meadow, the cow's in the corn;
Where is the boy that looks after the sheep?
He's under a haystack, fast asleep.
Will you wake him?
No, not I!
For if I do, he's sure to cry.

SEE-SAW, MARGERY DAW

See-saw, Margery Daw,
Jenny shall have a new master;
She shall have but a penny a day
Because she can't go any faster.

GIRLS AND BOYS COME OUT TO PLAY

Girls and boys come out to play
The moon it shines as bright as day.
Leave your supper and leave your sleep
And come with your playfellows into the street;
Come with a whoop and come with a call,
Come with a goodwill, or come not at all;
Up the ladder and down the wall,
A halfpenny loaf will serve us all.
You find milk and I'll find flour.
And we'll have pudding in half an hour.

LITTLE JUMPING JOAN

Here am I, little Jumping Joan;
When nobody's with me
I'm always alone.

AS I WAS GOING UP
PIPPIN HILL

As I was going up Pippin hill
Pippin hill was dirty.
There I met a pretty miss
And she dropped me a curtsey.

Little miss, pretty miss,
Blessings light upon you!
If I had half a crown a day
I'd gladly spend it on you.

LITTLE BETTY BLUE

Little Betty Blue
Lost her holiday shoe.
What will poor Betty do?
Why, give her another,
To match the other
And then she may walk in two.

LITTLE MAID, LITTLE MAID

Little maid, little maid
Whither goest thou?
Down to the meadow
To milk my cow.

TOM, HE WAS A PIPER'S SON

Tom, he was a piper's son
He learned to play when he was young,
And all the tune that he could play
Was 'Over the Hills and Far Away'.

HERE WE GO LOOBY-LOO

Here we go Looby-loo
Here we go Looby-light
Here we go Looby-loo
All on a Saturday night.

HERE WE GO ROUND
THE
MULBERRY BUSH

Here we go round the mulberry bush
The mulberry bush, the mulberry bush;
Here we go round the mulberry bush
On a cold and frosty morning.

This is the way we wash our clothes
This is the way we iron our clothes
This is the way we wash our hands
This is the way we do our hair
This is the way we go to school
This is the way we come home from school
On a cold and frosty morning.

LITTLE GIRL, LITTLE GIRL

'Little girl, little girl
Where have you been?'
'Gathering roses to give to the Queen.'
'Little girl, little girl
What did she give you?'
'She gave me a diamond as big as my shoe.'

THE ROSE IS RED,
THE ROSE IS WHITE

The rose is red, the rose is white
The rose is in my garden;
How could I part
With my sweetheart
For twopence halfpenny farthing?

ROSES ARE RED

Roses are red,
Violets are blue,
Sugar is sweet,
And so are you.

There Was An Old Woman
Who Lived In A Shoe

There was an old woman who lived in a shoe
She had so many children she didn't know what to do;
She gave them some broth without any bread
And smacked them all soundly and put them to bed.

LAVENDER'S BLUE, DILLY DILLY

Lavender's blue, dilly dilly, lavender's green,
When I am King, dilly dilly, you shall be Queen;
Call up your men, dilly dilly, set them to work,
Some to the plough, dilly dilly, some to the cart;
Some to make hay, dilly dilly, some to thresh corn,
While you and I, dilly dilly, keep ourselves warm.

BOBBY SHAFTO'S GONE TO SEA

Bobby Shafto's gone to sea
Silver buckles at his knee;
He'll come back and marry me;
Bonny Bobby Shaftoe.

Bobby Shafto's tall and fair
Combing down his yellow hair,
He's my love for every more;
Bonny Bobby Shafto.

BABIES

HUSH-A-BYE BABY
ON THE
TREE TOP

Hush-a-bye baby on the tree top,
When the wind blows
The cradle will rock;
When the bough breaks
The cradle will fall;
Down will come baby, cradle and all.

DANCE TO YOUR DADDY

Dance to your Daddy,
My little laddy,
Dance to your Daddy,
My little lamb.
You shall have a fishy
In a little dishy,
You shall have a fishy
When the boat comes home.

I HAVE BUILT
A
LITTLE HOUSE

I have built a little house
With a chimney tall;
A roof of red
A garden shed
And a garden wall.

The door is wide –
You can peep inside –
There's just enough room for two;
A little armchair
And a table, where
I've supper set for me and you.

HERE ARE MY LADY'S KNIVES AND FORKS

Here are my lady's knives and forks
Here is my lady's table;
This is my lady's looking glass
And here is the baby's cradle!

ROUND AND ROUND THE GARDEN

Round and round the garden
Like a teddy bear;
One step; two step –
Tickly under there!

ONCE I FOUND
AN APPLE PIP

Once I found an apple pip
And stuck it in the ground,
When I came to look at it
A tiny shoot I found.

The shoot grew up and up each day;
It soon became a tree.
I picked the rosy apples then
And ate them for my tea.

Hush, Little Baby, Don't Say a Word

Hush, little baby, don't say a word,
Daddy's going to buy you a mocking bird.
If that mocking bird don't sing,
Daddy's going to buy you a diamond ring.
If that diamond ring turns to brass,
Daddy's going to buy you a looking glass.
If that looking glass gets broke
Daddy's going to buy you a billy goat.
If that billy goat runs away –
Daddy'll buy you another, today.

ROCK-A-BYE BABY

Rock-a-bye baby
Your cradle is green;
Father's a nobleman
Mother's a queen.
Betty's a lady
And wears a gold ring;
And Johnny's a drummer
That drums for the King.

I Can Tie My Shoe Lace

I can tie my shoe lace
I can comb my hair
I can wash my hands and face
And dry myself with care.

I can brush my teeth, too,
And button up my frocks;
I can say, 'How do you do?'
And put on both my socks.

HUSH MY DOLLY, MY BABY DON'T CRY

Hush my dolly, my baby don't cry!
I'll give you bread and some milk, by and by.
Or perhaps you like custard, or maybe a tart?
Then to either you're welcome, with all my whole heart.

TWO YOUNG LADIES

Two young ladies met in a lane;
Bowed most politely, bowed once again,
How do you do? How do you do?
How do you do again?

CUCKOO, CUCKOO, CHERRY TREE

Cuckoo, cuckoo, cherry tree,
Catch a bird and give it to me;
Let the tree be high or low
Sunshine, wind or rain or snow.

SLEEP, BABY, SLEEP

Sleep, baby, sleep,
Our cottage vale is deep;
A little lamb is on the green
His woolly fleece is soft and clean.
Sleep, baby, sleep.